THE MISSING TOOTH MYSTERY

By Maria S. Barbo

Illustrated by Duendes del Sur

Hello Reader — Level 1

15 14 13   7 8 9/0

Designed by Maria Stasavage
Printed in the U.S.A.
First Scholastic printing, February 2002

SCHOLASTIC INC.

New York   Toronto   London   Auckland   Sydney
Mexico City   New Delhi   Hong Kong   Buenos Aires

and the gang were playing

at their friends' .

, , and were

playing with a .

and sat at the

and ate.

They ate .

They chomped on an .

They drank a lot of .

and were happy.

Their friend, Billy, ran up to  and  .

"I lost my  !" he said.

"Like, that's great!" said  .

"The  might bring you  ."

"No, I don't know where my  is," said Billy.

"  and I will find your missing  ," said  .

Clankedy, clank, whir, whir.

"What's that noise?" asked  .

"Zoinks! It sounds like a monster

!"

"Ronster ?!" was

scared. Super scared.

"We have to be brave," told

. "We have a to find."

"Before I lost my ," said Billy,

"I was digging in the 🌼."

Was Billy's 🦷 under the 🌼?

Maybe the 🦷 fell into the

🕳.

🐕 dug up the 🌼.

🧑 looked in the 🕳.

They did not see the 🦷. But

they heard a funny noise.

Clankedy, clank, whir, whir.

"The monster  found us!"

"Run!" said  .

Shaggy and Scooby ran back to

the  .

They stopped for some

and 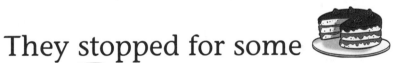 .

Trying to find the missing

was hard work.

"Before I dug in the , I slid down the ," said Billy.

Was Billy's on the ?

slid down the .

searched the .

They did not find the missing . But they heard a funny noise.

Clankedy, clank, whir, whir.

"Rikes! !" yelled .

hopped on Billy's .

and rode the

all around the .

They rode the far away

from the monster .

"Before I rode my , I ate an ," said Billy. And I played with my , and my toy ."

 looked under the .

 took a close look at the .

They did not find the missing . But they heard a funny noise.

Clankedy, clank, whir, whir.

"It is the monster !"

shouted .

"?!" said . "Ruh-roh!"

 tossed the .

The  hit .

 lost her .

"Jinkies!" said . "What is

that funny noise?"

and hid under a

 .

 put on her 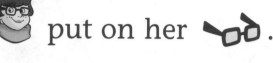 .

"It is not a monster 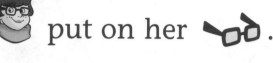 ,"

said .

"It is my toy 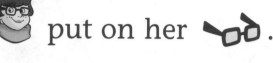 ," said Billy.

"The toy  has your  !"

said  .

"Now I can put my  under my ," said Billy.

"And the  will visit you," said .

 was proud of  and .

 and  gave them .

"Thanks  and ," said Billy.

"Scooby-Dooby-Doo!" barked .

Did you spot all the picture clues in this Scooby-Doo mystery?

Each picture clue is on a flash card. Ask a grown-up to cut out the flash cards. Then try reading the words on the back of the cards. The pictures will be your clue.

Reading is fun with Scooby-Doo!